For my father-in-law, Antonio, his son,
Pierluigi, and my sons, Peter and Max —K. B.

For Anne and Salomé —G. H.

SQUARE
FISH
An Imprint of Macmillan

Library of Congress Cataloging-in-Publication Data
Banks, Kate, 1960–
The night worker / Kate Banks ; pictures by Georg Hallensleben.
p.   cm.
Summary: Alex wants to be a "night worker" like his father
who goes to work at a construction site after Alex goes to bed.
ISBN 978-0-374-40000-2
[1. Night—Fiction. 2. Work—Fiction. 3. Construction workers—
Fiction. 4. Fathers and sons—Fiction.]
I. Hallensleben, Georg, ill. II. Title.
PZ7.B22594Ni 2000   [E]—dc21   99-27595

Originally published in the United States by Farrar Straus Giroux
First Square Fish Edition: June 2012
Square Fish logo designed by Filomena Tuosto
mackids.com

10 9

AR: 2.3 / LEXILE: AD 260L

Kate Banks

The Night Worker

Pictures by Georg Hallensleben

SQUARE
FISH

Farrar Straus Giroux
New York

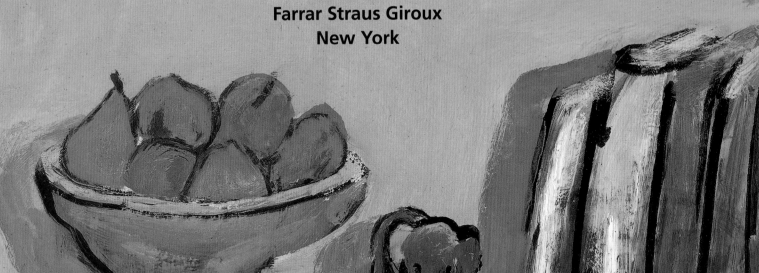

Night falls. Bedtime comes.
Papa kisses Alex good night.
Then he puts on his hard hat.
He is an engineer. And he is a night worker.
"Take me with you," whispers Alex.
"Not tonight," says Papa.

Then one night Papa has a surprise.
A hard hat for Alex.
Alex puts it on and smiles.
"Come on," says Papa.
And while Mama sleeps, Alex and Papa
head quietly into the night.

A street sweeper is making his rounds.
A delivery man parks his truck.
He stops to talk to a policewoman.
"They are night workers, too," says Papa.
"I want to be a night worker," says Alex.

Papa pulls into the construction site.
Alex hears the rattle and clang of heavy machinery.
Men are hollowing out the earth.
A building is going up.

Papa and Alex switch on their flashlights.
And as they survey the work site,
stars shine like beacons for the night workers.

Papa stops to talk to the foreman.
He spreads out a plan of the project.
"We're digging here," he says.
He points to a bulldozer leveling the ground.
Clouds rise from the dust as a steel shovel
pushes soil into a midnight mountain.

An excavator rumbles and turns.
It reaches its giant arm into the air and waves.
Alex waves back. Then it sinks its teeth into the earth
and lets out a groan like a giant rolling over in bed.

In a corner a cement mixer hums steadily.
Men are pouring concrete and sealing off the earth.
"They are laying the foundation," says Papa.

He hoists Alex onto a railing.
A crane moves its mammoth load
across the sky while someone
keeps watch from a booth overhead.

"I want to help," says Alex.
A big yellow loader starts its engine.
"Up you go," says Papa.
He sets Alex down beside the driver.

Slowly, they crawl along the gravel.
The driver puts Alex's hands on the levers.
"Ready?" he says. Alex nods and pushes down.

"I'm a night worker, too," Alex says, emptying his load.
The dump truck closes its gate and drives off.
A whistle sounds. Gears grind to a halt.
It's time for the night workers to take a break.

Papa and Alex survey the site one last time.
All motion is stopped like a held breath.

Papa lifts Alex into his arms.
"I'm tired," says Alex.
And they head back into the night.
A couple stands under a streetlight.
A woman is walking a dog.

It is late.
Alex takes off his hard hat.
He pulls on his pajamas
and crawls into bed.

Morning comes.
And while the city wakes, a little boy sleeps
and dreams of being a night worker.